The Boy
Who Stole
the Elephant

by JULILLY H. KOHLER

Illustrated by Lee Ames

Cover by Richard Amundsen

SCHOLASTIC BOOK SERVICES

NEW YORK • TORONTO • LONDON • AUCKLAND • SYDNEY

Copyright 1952 by Julilly H. Kohler. This edition is published by Scholastic Book Services, a division of Scholastic Magazines, Inc., by arrangement with Alfred A. Knopf, Inc.

5th printing.................December 1970

Printed in the U.S.A.

For
RICHARD COOK WALLER
Cousin, Uncle, Godfather, Inspiration
whose ear is always tuned to a
tall tale from Kentucky!

CHAPTER ONE

THIS IS the story of a boy who stole an elephant. That sounds like a pretty tall tale, but it really happened, believe it or not! It happened about fifty years ago near a sleepy little town in Western Kentucky, not far from the Ohio River. Crosstown, it was called; not because the people were cranky, but because the river narrowed right there, and there were lots of sandbars where wagon-trains and settlers going West in the early days could find a shallow place to cross over into Illinois.

The boy's name was Gyp, like the first part of gypsy, which wasn't a bad name for this boy. He was dark, like a gypsy, and wiry and strong, even though he didn't have much fat on his bones. He didn't have a father or mother, and he had lived most of his twelve years with a kind of relative, named Mr. Catfish Williams. (Everybody called him that, so it must have been his name!)

Mr. Catfish Williams was the owner of a third-rate circus, and Gyp lived with him and helped to run it, for his board and keep. Mr. Catfish Williams was very fond of talking, but he wasn't fond of work, so Gyp really did a lot of the running! Of course, it wasn't a very big circus. It had only one tent with one ring and one clown and no band, just a calliope wagon. There was one couple, the Waverleys, who did acrobatic tricks on the trapeze and highwire; and two others, Mr. Mogg and his sister, who rode bareback and had the trained dogs and the ponies. They were even less fond of work than Mr. Catfish Williams. Gyp was kept pretty busy.

When they got to a little town where the circus would play for two or three days, Mr. Catfish Williams would say, "You, Gyp! Run in to the courthouse square, find a few husky fellows who'd like to help set up the tent and benches."

Mrs. Waverley would stick her head out the door of her wagon and call, "Oh, Gyp, bring me back a loaf of bread and a nickel's worth of ice."

Then, when he got back, one of the Moggs, or maybe the clown, who never smiled even when he had his costume and paint on, would find out he needed the water pails filled, or the kindling chopped, or the horses fed. And Mr. Catfish Williams had taught Gyp, from the time he was a little fellow, to stir up the corn pone and put on the bacon or the greens or whatever there was going to be for dinner.

Gyp didn't really mind the work. Oh, he got a little tired, especially about late August when it was so hot and sticky that he couldn't sleep at night. He'd take his old pallet and quilt out of the front of the calliope wagon which was his quarters, and stretch out on the ground to get a little breeze. He'd listen to the locusts and the katydids, which meant another hot day tomorrow, and watch the stars climb over the tent and slide down the other side. Gyp minded the lonesomeness more than the work, for he never had the feeling that he really belonged to anybody. But he wouldn't have minded either of those things if only it had been a first-class circus!

Gyp couldn't bear driving the calliope wagon in

a parade that hardly had twenty people watching it march down Main Street. It made him squirm to have to tell the big town boys to put up just five rows of benches! Ponies and dogs and acrobats and even pink cotton candy weren't enough to make most people pay out fifty cents and sit in a dusty sticky tent in the middle of summer.

Business was bad and Gyp knew it. That was worse than being tired or lonesome. That could mean being hungry, too!

"If we only had a menagerie," whispered Gyp, shifting around on the hard ground to get a glimpse of a star just over the tent pole. "Lions, maybe, or at least a bear. That would get the people in! They'd drive ten miles after chores to see wild animals!" He thought longingly of the posters he'd seen of the big Jeffreys' Jewels Circuses . . . the jungle, the mystery of faraway lands. Those would be circuses worth working for!

The summer Gyp was twelve, his dream came true. It was early June, and they were in Paducah, setting up the wagons and waiting for the rest of the crew to start another season. Mr. Catfish Williams had been gone all day on business, but Gyp never expected the news he brought back with him.

"You, Gyp!" called Mr. Catfish Williams, from

the foot of the steps of his wagon, where Gyp was starting to fix supper. "Leave that cookin', and run get the hammer and an iron stake and that big chain we used last year when the wagon fell in the creek. And keep an eye peeled for the big wagon from Jeffreys' Jewels."

Gyp's heart began to pound. "Jeffreys' Jewels' wagon, sir? The big three-ring circus?"

"It ain't so all-fired big! Now run! Tom Jeffreys is comin' out to do some business with us. Mustn't keep the great man waitin'!"

Gyp was panting as he dragged the rusty stake and chain and the ten-pound roustabout sledge hammer over to Mr. Catfish Williams. But the thought of Mr. Tom Jeffreys gave him strength.

"He's a good friend of yours, isn't he, Mr. Catfish Williams?"

"He ought to be! Rode wild hosses together with Buffalo Bill twenty years ago. Pound that stake in the ground right here, Gyp. And pound it in good." Mr. Catfish Williams sat down on the steps of his wagon and helped himself to a big "chew" off the twist of tobacco he always kept in his coat pocket. His eyes narrowed. "Jeffreys' Jewels, my foot! In them days he didn't have any more money in his pocket than I did. No pride, either. Didn't

care what kind of work he did, just so it paid him
a dime."

Gyp rested his arms for a minute. "Are you going
to chain up some wild horses here, Mr. Catfish
Williams? Is Mr. Jeffreys going to give us some for
a new act?"

Squatch! ! Mr. Catfish Williams squirted a stream
of tobacco juice right at Gyp's sledge hammer. Gyp
hurriedly swung at the stake. "*Give*, my foot! I
didn't go beggin' from Tom Jeffreys. Let him have
his string of circuses, and his chain of cheap restaurants and his high-toned friends up at Frank-
fort! I guess all his luck helps him forget his hard
times. A loan, he calls it, and he laughs! 'The kind
of loan you'll have to pay back—this time,' he
says!"

The sound of wagon wheels rumbling came just
in time. Gyp didn't like the look on Mr. Catfish
Williams' face. He had seen it many times before,
and it meant trouble for somebody, usually Gyp!

"Why, it's the No. 1 menagerie wagon! And Mr.
Jeffreys is riding alongside on Star. Is he lending
us some wild animals, Mr. Catfish Williams?"

Mr. Catfish Williams rose. He shifted his tobacco
from one unshaven cheek to the other, took off his
battered hat, wiped the sweaty band with a red-
dotted handkerchief, then put his hat back on. His

eyes never left the figure on the handsome white horse that was being forced to curb its prancing to keep pace with the huge gold and crimson wagon. Mr. Tom Jeffreys still rode as if he were in the center ring with a spotlight on him.

"My generous old friend," said Mr. Catfish Williams, with a most unpleasant smile, "is lendin' us *one* animal for the season, to help us get on our feet. Here." He pulled a folded paper from his rumpled seersucker coat and thrust it at Gyp. "Pick up the rest of these handbills at the printer's tomorrow. See that they git handed out in every town we play. Now go on back and start supper. Don't be hangin' around."

Gyp streaked up the steps of the wagon, and slammed the door. Inside, he looked in awe at the picture on the paper in his hand.

QUEENIE—BIGGEST LIVING THING IN THE WORLD.

Gyp looked at the picture, then he tiptoed over, and very quietly opened the door of the wagon just enough of a crack to peek through. The menagerie wagon had stopped now. It was as big as a freight train, and decorated from top to wheels with swirling painted figures and streamers. Across the side, the bold black letters announced to the world that this was Menagerie Wagon No. 1 of the DIAMOND CIRCUS OF JEFFREYS' JEWELS, THE GREATEST STRING OF CIRCUSES ON EARTH. It took Gyp's breath away. It towered above the faded old calliope wagon just as the man on the white horse towered above Mr. Catfish Williams.

But both of them, and the whole world, seemed dwarfed by the size of the elephant which was slowly, majestically, coming down the gangplank of the wagon. For once Mr. Catfish Williams' poster had told the truth! Queenie was well named. Her head was noble, broad as a mountain, with ears that hung like flags on the big top when the breeze is slack. The feet she placed so surely, almost daintily, were as big round as a center tent pole, and her huge flanks rocked like some grey stone building that has suddenly and crazily decided to move from its foundations.

"Glory!" whispered Gyp. "I didn't need to pound in that measly iron stake. Isn't she wonderful!"

He hardly felt his hand on the wagon door, or his feet going down the steps. He just suddenly found himself walking over to Mr. Jeffreys and holding Star's bridle while Mr. Jeffreys swung down. He gave a short whistle and Queenie walked

dutifully over and let Mr. Jeffreys snap a chain to a ring in the wide iron band around her left front leg and then fasten it around a big oak tree. With one hand, he motioned to Mr. Catfish Williams; the other he kept on Queenie's vast side. Every now and then he would double up his fist and beat a little rhythm: one-two; one-two-three, which Queenie seemed to know and respond to.

Gyp's eyes widened. Mr. Jeffreys might be a man who wasn't too proud to work for a dime but he certainly was mighty fine looking. He wore his hair long, just like Buffalo Bill. It was white and clean-scrubbed and set off the dark tanned skin of his face. He was tall and straight as an Indian and his eyes looked at Mr. Catfish Williams in a way that made Gyp glad he wasn't looking at him. He spoke in a low voice, but Gyp could hear every word as plain as if he were shouting.

"Well, there she is, Catfish. Remember what I said about her food. A bale of hay and five bushels of oats a day, do you understand? This elephant is used to kings and princes . . . and I won't have her starved or mistreated. None of your sawdust tricks, Catfish . . ."

"Why, Tom!" The protesting voice was so humble that Gyp wouldn't have believed it was Mr. Catfish Williams if he hadn't seen his jaws moving.

"You know what an animal lover I've always been, Tom. I will care for Queenie as if she was my own."

"That's just what I'm afraid of," said Mr. Jeffreys, with a funny kind of smile. "She was headed for the big-time circuit, but she had a little upset and I wouldn't risk her health. That's why she's available for your show this summer. The quiet will be good for her."

Gyp could see the red flush rising up into Mr. Catfish Williams' face.

"No offense meant, Catfish. I'm glad to help you out. But I want you to understand what kind of an elephant you've got here. No royal elephant ever walked the dusty roads of Kentucky before. And never might again. Don't care for Queenie as if she were your own, Catfish! Care for her as if she were mine!"

Mr. Jeffreys suddenly seemed to see Gyp standing there, holding Star's reins. He rested his strong, brown hand on Gyp's shoulder for a second and looked straight into Gyp's eyes. Then he smiled, and beat a little rhythm on Gyp's arm: one-two; one-two-three, as if Gyp belonged to him, just like Queenie.

"Here's a good elephant boy, Catfish," he said. "Let him take care of Queenie!" Then he swung himself lightly into his saddle. The silver trappings chattered and danced. Queenie gave a little snuffling snort and swung her trunk up to Mr. Jeffreys. "Goodbye, Queenie. Be a good girl. I'll come get you on Labor Day." The white horse swung round and was gone in a rush of dust and wind and silver.

"Glory!" whispered Gyp. He looked at Queenie, then at Mr. Catfish Williams. The dust swirled around and settled, but Mr. Catfish Williams did not move a muscle. He kept his eyes on the man and the horse until they disappeared around a pecan grove at the turn of the road. Then, slowly, deliberately, Mr. Catfish Williams walked over toward Queenie. He shifted his wad of tobacco and looked her over, from head to foot. Then, *squatch!* Gyp saw a stream of tobacco juice shoot squarely at Queenie's trunk. It ran in horrid little streams down to the sensitive tip and off into the dust at her feet. Queenie did not move. Then Mr. Catfish Williams turned and looked at Gyp.

"Didn't I tell you to go start supper? Now, git. And don't let me catch you touchin' a finger to that elephant. I mean what I say."

Gyp leaped up the wagon steps and began to shake up the stove inside. He was breathing so hard his chest hurt. He would slip out after a while and wash the nasty-smelling stuff off Queenie, no mat-

ter what happened. He trembled to think how mad
Mr. Tom Jeffreys would be if he had seen that, but
he had a feeling in his bones that was why Mr. Catfish Williams did it.

"He didn't like Mr. Jeffreys telling me to take
care of Queenie. I reckon I'll have to keep my eyes
peeled to look out for her this summer. So Mr.
Jeffreys will be proud of her . . . and me, when he
comes for her on Labor Day."

Gyp's heart suddenly swelled with happiness as
he remembered Mr. Jeffreys' hand on his shoulder.
Queenie was beautiful! Mr. Jeffreys couldn't be too
hard a man, if a royal elephant was that fond of
him!

"A royal elephant! And she's ours for all summer. This is going to be a real circus now!"

CHAPTER TWO

GYP'S first chance to look after Queenie came sooner than he expected, on the very opening day of the circus. They had all crossed the Ohio on the ferryboat at Paducah, and were headed for the little river towns of Illinois, instead of playing Kentucky as they usually did. Gyp suspected Mr. Catfish Williams had changed his plans just for spite. First, so he wouldn't run any chance of meeting Mr. Tom Jeffreys, who was always traveling around the state, and, second, so those words of his wouldn't come true. So far, "No royal elephant had yet walked the dusty roads of Kentucky."

14

Everybody was ready. Everything was set up. Gyp had papered the board fences with posters, and stuffed handbills in all the screen doors in town. If every man, woman, and child in that town didn't know that "Queenie, the Biggest Living Thing in the World" was going to appear that day, it was because they were all stone blind!

Gyp was aching to polish up Queenie's toenails, and scrub her huge sides with a broom, but Mr. Catfish Williams had given strict orders that nobody but himself was to go near Queenie. And Gyp knew he would ache across the seat of his pants if he disobeyed. So every day he did his other work, and watched Queenie, and fretted and fretted.

For the truth of the matter was, Queenie didn't like Mr. Catfish Williams. Oh, she got her food every day, and she went where she was told, but she would get restless every time Mr. Catfish Williams came near her. If she even saw him open his wagon door and come down the steps when it was time for her dinner or her exercise, she would begin to rock from one foot to the other, not contentedly, but uneasily. If he laid his hand on her side, she would rattle her chain and shuffle her feet, as if to say, "If I really wanted to, I could snap this like a clover chain!"

Finally, on the very morning of the opening parade, there was trouble. Gyp had harnessed the horses and built up the steam in the old calliope, so it was all ready to play. The wagons and ponies were all lined up. All they needed now was Queenie to start the parade. But Queenie wouldn't start. Queenie didn't like Mr. Catfish Williams any better just because he had his parade uniform on. She wouldn't stir one step from under her tree.

"Blast you!" shouted Mr. Catfish Williams. "Get movin', there. Everything's ready! How can we have a parade, if you stand there as stubborn as a mule!"

Queenie opened her big ears part way and rocked restlessly. Mr. Catfish Williams set his big sweaty palms against Queenie's sides. It was like a fly pushing against a hill.

"Git up! Git! I'll take a hook to you. Royal, my foot! You're a crazy fool elephant and Tom Jeffreys played me for a sucker. Here I'm feedin' you a dollar's worth of feed a day and you won't even lead a parade. Where's my bull whip? I'll show you . . ."

Gyp could bear it no longer. "Oh, wait! Wait!" He ran out from behind the calliope wagon and pulled at the furious man's arm. "You can't whip Queenie, Mr. Catfish Williams. Why, Queenie's used to kings and princes! She'll come along, I know she will!"

Gyp wasn't as sure as he sounded. He'd never really touched an elephant before, and Queenie was still pretty upset. Her big ears were wide open as wings and her little eyes glittered so far above Gyp that he couldn't tell whether there was any friendliness in them or not. He pulled Mr. Catfish Williams away from Queenie, then dug his hand down in his overall pocket for a peanut. Slowly he walked toward her, hand outstretched.

"Hi, Queenie. Hi, Queenie, girl," he said softly. "You don't have to worry, Queenie, it's just a parade and you're going to be the leader. You like to lead parades, don't you, Queenie? That's what you did for the kings and princes, I'll bet."

Queenie stopped her rocking and stood very still. Gyp took a few steps closer. "Sure, Queenie. You'll be the leader. Everybody'll look at you and I'll be so proud that you're in our circus. Mr. Jeffreys'll be proud, too, Queenie. Want a peanut?"

Slowly, slowly, Queenie's great ears floated down like two big birds. She lowered her head till Gyp could really see her eyes. They twinkled at Gyp like a child who'd been showing off before company and knew she'd been found out. Gyp put out his left hand and stroked the thick, grey wrinkled trunk while he still offered the peanut on his right.

The round flat end of Queenie's trunk wobbled and snuffled, then came curling round and sniffed at Gyp. Then it sniffed at his hand, and the peanut disappeared like magic!

Gyp snickered and twisted his bare toes in the dirt. "That tickles!" he said, and he doubled up his fist and beat on Queenie's tall sides as hard as he could: one-two; one-two-three.

Queenie tucked the peanut neatly under her upper lip and chewed contentedly. With Gyp's hand on her side she walked docilely beside him toward the head of the wagons, and made a little snuffling sound as she went.

Squatch! "Two of a kind," growled Mr. Catfish Williams.

When the parade went down Main Street, the sidewalks were packed and jammed. Queenie led the parade, all right, and leading Queenie, with the proud step of the mightiest Rajah of the Indies, was Gyp. Mr. Catfish Williams drove the calliope!

"Look at that crowd, Queenie," shouted Gyp, above the noise. "We're a real circus now!"

And they were. With Queenie in the show, everything was different. So many people turned out for the night performance that Mr. Catfish Williams had to borrow more benches from the base-

ball team! When they moved to the next town, the clown thought up some new tricks and painted his smile up instead of down! They stayed there a whole week so the Waverleys shortened the ropes of their trapezes and began to practice their one and a half somersault that they hadn't bothered to do for a handful of audience! Everything got better—except Queenie and Mr. Catfish Williams. She wouldn't let him near her unless Gyp was with him, and the more she liked Gyp, the more Mr. Catfish Williams disliked both of them.

"You, Gyp!" said Mr. Catfish Williams, the night they were pulling up stakes, and heading for their Fourth of July engagement. "From now on you're in charge of this elephant."

Gyp forgot everything but his joy. "Honest, Mr. Catfish Williams? You mean feed her and everything?"

"I mean everything. So don't be neglectin' the hosses, and the wagon-cleanin', and candy stands. If you and this overgrown mule are so all-fired crazy about each other, I might as well get a little help out of you. You both eat twice your weight in work as it is!"

Gyp bit his tongue to keep his temper. He watched Mr. Catfish Williams pull a big black cigar from the pocket of his new white linen suit and strike a match with his thumb nail. He noticed a new ring set with a big red stone on his finger and smelled the fancy hair tonic he had gotten uptown. Business was certainly picking up. The money was rolling in, but so far nobody but Mr. Catfish Williams had even gotten a good look at it. Mr. Catfish Williams wore his hair long now, like Mr. Tom Jeffreys, but it still was dank and stringy, and his fingernails were still dirty. Gyp wondered what Mr. Catfish Williams would do next summer when he had to go back to the measly business of running his circus without Queenie.

"Without Queenie?" Gyp caught his breath. For the first time in his life he thought about his future. What would he do next summer, or all the rest of his life! "I sure won't spend it with Mr. Catfish Williams!" he promised Queenie, as he led her off to the all-night move through the hot, quiet, summer night to their next town.

From then on Gyp's lonely days were gone. He loved Queenie like some boys would love their whole big family of aunts and uncles and cousins on both sides! He didn't care how much other work there was, he kept her wash bucket filled with clean drinking water, even if he had to walk a mile to the river or the town pump. He knew just how much to feed her: hadn't Mr. Tom Jeffreys said so himself? One bale of hay and five bushels of oats a day. And on extra hot days he dragged a pitchfork over to scratch up the dirt for Queenie so she could give herself a dust bath to cool off. Queenie meant the world to Gyp.

And as for Queenie, she acted like a silly old hen with one chick! No matter how late it was by the time Gyp got through his work at night, Queenie waited up for him. She wouldn't lie down until he dragged his pallet over under her tree. Then she'd drop to her knees and let herself down right beside him, and if she'd been a foot closer she'd have smashed him flat as a pancake! Gyp would reach over and double up his fist and pound on her side: one-two; one-two-three, and they'd both go to sleep, happy.

The long, hot summer days rolled by. August was a scorcher with no rain for three weeks running. The circus was swinging round toward home now, working back to a good place to cross the river into Kentucky. Every day the sun blazed down on the corn in the river bottom lands, and it grew ripe and sweet. But the wind that blew across them was like a blast furnace, and the nights were as thick with the choking heat as the days.

Good circus weather, everybody said. Might as well be hot at the circus as at home! And wasn't that Queenie wonderful, the way she minded that little boy? So the crowds still poured in, and Mr. Catfish Williams still took in all the money. The last week of the season the clown and the Waverleys and the Moggs and the roustabouts felt the heat, too, and began to complain about their salaries. To everybody's surprise, Mr. Catfish Williams didn't get either hot or annoyed. He just listened to the complaints, and twiddled his new red ring, and smoked his black cigar.

"You're right; you're absolutely right. It's been a good season and you're entitled to more money. I'm keepin' strict accounts and when we get back to Paducah next week, you'll all get your pay plus a share of the profits. Does that suit you?"

It did. But it surprised them, too. And it surprised Gyp most of all. He'd been wakened two nights in a row by talk in Mr. Catfish Williams' wagon, and on this Saturday night he saw a short, fat man with a cane come out of the wagon, still talking. The words were spoken in a whisper, but Gyp's ears were sharp.

"You're sure she's good-natured? With so many children coming to a zoo, we have to have one that's good-natured."

Mr. Catfish Williams put his arm around the little fat man's shoulders, and pointed over to Gyp. Gyp froze as still as a shadow as they walked a little closer. "Take a look at that! Sleeps right next to my own little son! Think I'd allow that if she didn't have the disposition of an angel?"

Gyp heard the man's answer rustle back to him faintly, as they moved along the beaten path. "Then it's a deal. I'll have the papers drawn up Monday morning, and bring you the money by the time the evening performance is over. Our freight train will load Queenie on at midnight and she'll be in her new Chicago home before she knows it. I can't tell you how happy we will be to have her. She's the finest specimen I've ever seen."

Gyp's head rocked with horror. Was he dreaming? Did his ears play him tricks, with all the tree toads croaking? Quick as a monkey, he darted up from his pallet and into the shadows of the wagons. He slid from one to the other until he was next to Mr. Catfish Williams' own steps. His heart pounded so hard that he was afraid the two men could hear it. But they were still deep in their own discussion. Mr. Catfish Williams was arguing about something.

"It's very simple. Nothin' to worry about. The boy there can load Queenie on the train as well as

I can. You've seen him in the ring with her. I happen to have some urgent business in Atlanta on Monday, and have to catch the Sunday noon train out of here. You bring the money at ten tomorrow mornin', and I'll give you the receipt. Then you can come back for her Monday evenin', just like we planned. Ain't that reasonable? I'd gladly stay to help you load her, only this is a very important matter, and there's only one train south out of here a day."

The fat man jabbed his cane in the hard-baked ground. "I suppose it's all right. My own trainer'll be along, too. All right, then. I'll bring the money tomorrow morning."

"Fine. I'll walk to the road with you. This path is pretty full of roots to trip on."

Gyp streaked back to Queenie's side. He could hardly breathe, but not from running. Not from the heat, either. What took his breath away was the awful thought of Mr. Tom Jeffreys' face when he came for Queenie on Labor Day and she was gone. Gone . . . to a zoo in Chicago! Gone for nobody knows how much money . . . and the money would be gone, too, in Mr. Catfish Williams' thieving pockets!

"He wouldn't dare! He can't sell Queenie, if she belongs to Mr. Jeffreys. He could be put in jail for that!" Then Gyp remembered what he had heard the man saying. If Mr. Catfish Williams was scoundrel enough to sell Queenie, he could make out ownership papers that looked real. Nobody would take a boy's word against those papers. If only he could get to Mr. Tom Jeffreys! But there wasn't time!

CHAPTER THREE

THE SOUND of steps along the path made Gyp
flop down beside Queenie. He watched Mr. Catfish Williams go up his steps and into his wagon.
In a few minutes the lamp went out, and all was
dark and quiet. Mr. Catfish Williams would have
pleasant dreams tonight, for all his plans were
working. By this time tomorrow night he would be
through with circuses and elephants for good! He'd
have money in his pocket, and better than money
. . . he would get even with Tom Jeffreys.

27

"He's always hated Mr. Jeffreys," thought Gyp, "because Mr. Jeffreys is a worker. And Mr. Catfish Williams is shiftless. And mean. He doesn't care what happens to the rest of the circus people. He'll take all that money he promised to divide with them in Paducah!"

Suddenly Gyp had an idea so crazy that it made him feel light-headed. He sat straight up on his old pallet and took a deep breath. What if Queenie wasn't here tomorrow morning. Mr. Catfish Williams couldn't sell her then, could he? A deep, quiet voice seemed to speak in his mind: "Here's a good elephant boy . . . Let him take care of Queenie."

Gyp's spine tingled. Mr. Tom Jeffreys was depending on him! If he and Queenie could get across the river to Kentucky before daylight, they'd have a good chance of being safe!

As if he had spoken aloud, Queenie snuffled and stirred. Gyp leaped to her side and whispered to her softly, "Up, Queenie, up, girl." He patted her trunk soothingly. "Quiet now, Queenie. Don't make a noise. We haven't a chance if he wakes up."

Like a part of the earth itself moving, the mammoth grey body shuddered, then rolled over and rose. In the dim starlight, Queenie looked like a mountain on the move. Gyp dared not stop to think ahead, or his nerve would fail him. He knew Mr. Catfish Williams would be after him like a bloodhound as soon as he found them gone. "We've got three or four hours, Queenie, for a head start. It's only about ten miles to the river. We're opposite Crosstown, and that's the shallowest spot between here and Paducah. Lucky for us there hasn't been a rain for ages. Once we're over to the Kentucky side, Queenie, we'll be all right. I know we will. Mr. Jeffreys is going to be in Paducah on Labor Day, and I'm going to see he finds you waiting for him. No Chicago zoo is going to get you, Queenie. You can bet your bottom dollar on that!"

Queenie swung her trunk happily from side to side. Anything was all right with her, as long as Gyp was there. She didn't know just what was going on, but she smelled excitement, and that was all right, too. When she felt Gyp's hard little fist on her side: one-two; one-two-three, she swung out from under her tree for the last time, and walked happily at Gyp's side across the circus lot. When he whispered, "Wait a minute," she stopped dead, and watched him tiptoe into the calliope wagon. He was out in half a minute, wrapping a loaf of bread, a slab of cold barbecued mutton, and a bag of peanuts in a cloth.

"I can't carry hay or oats, Queenie, but we'll find plenty of corn in the cornfields. We won't starve. Here, you carry this." He thrust a stick through the twist of cloth and handed it up to Queenie, who curled her trunk around it obediently. "Come on now, we've got to hurry."

Past the wagons they went. Past the drowsing ponies, past the clown's quarters; past the Waverleys' and the Moggs'. Gyp wondered what they would think when they woke up in the morning and found him gone. He wished he could have left them a message telling why he'd run away, and warning them to get their money from Mr. Catfish Williams before he left town. "I guess they'll all think I'm stealing Queenie for myself! Maybe they'll help try to find me and turn me over to the law. But Mr. Jeffreys will believe me, I know he will. If I can only get to Mr. Jeffreys."

The sky was already lighter as they left the town behind them and came out on the rough, dusty river road. Nobody used it now except people who had their farms in the river bottoms. There wasn't any ferry here, and the water was too shallow for much fishing for catfish. Only the dark, old sycamores and hickory trees remembered the wagon trains of fifty years before that had jounced west along this trail after crossing the

river. There were tangled banks of wild honey-
suckle on either side, but their leaves were thick
with dust, and even in the waning night air there
was no freshness.

Once safely on the road, Gyp stopped Queenie.
He took the bundle from her trunk and gave a little
whistle. Queenie looked at Gyp and snorted. She
dropped down on her front knees, curled her
trunk for Gyp to step on, then ... *whish* ... he was
up on her broad flat head and sliding back onto
her shoulders. Queenie rocked up to her feet
again, and they were off. "This beats walking,"
said Gyp, "now, go, Queenie. Go as fast as you
can!"

Off went Queenie! That old covered wagon trail
had seen many a sight in its day, but never anything like the way the biggest elephant in captivity
trotted down it through the early dawn with a half-
scared gypsy of a boy on his back!

It was a good thing Gyp had grown up in coun-
try like this. Even though he had never been on
this side of the river before, it was so like the Kentucky shore that he knew in his bones which turns
to take. He knew, too, when they came up a little
rise, that the river lay ahead of them, even
though it was still too dark to make out the shore.

"We're here, Queenie! You're better than any

race horse up in Lexington! If we can get across the river before sunup we can find a place to hide till night time again." Queenie quickened her steps as she smelled the river water. It had been a dusty ride and she was thirsty. "Hey, Queenie, stop! Let me down. I've got to find a place for us to cross."

Gyp scrambled up on Queenie's head and slid down her trunk to the ground. His bones ached from the hard bumping he had taken on their flight. "I know now why those kings and princes always sit in little houses on their elephants," said Gyp, rubbing himself. "You're no feather bed, Queenie!"

Somehow a feather bed made him think of Mr. Catfish Williams! And a little chill of fear ran through Gyp's veins. He'd better hurry, before somebody at the circus woke up and began to look for them. They weren't out of danger yet . . . only the river could help them.

But the river didn't seem very helpful, either. It was low, very low, from the drought, and that was lucky. But the banks were steep and full of gullies and roots and rocks. Branches left by the receding water scraped at Gyp's legs in the dim starlight; his bare toes ached from the rocks; there was a muddy, fishy smell hanging over everything. His eyes ached from straining to find a good place to cross.

He went back to Queenie and untied the bundle. "How about a few peanuts, old girl? It's a little early for breakfast, but you've got a wetting ahead of you, and you'll need some nourishment."

He poured the peanuts out on the ground and Queenie began to pick them up daintily and eat them. Gyp pulled off a hunk of the bread and meat and started up the other way along the bank. Was he imagining it, or had the sky brightened? Seems as if he could make out the edge of the bank a lot easier. There! That looked like a place!

He picked his way over the stumps and sticks and climbed carefully down the bank. It looked pretty good—firm enough for Queenie to walk on. At the edge of the water, Gyp hesitated. Should he take off his shirt and pants? Could he hold 'em up out of the water on Queenie's back so they would be dry to put on when he reached the other side? Suddenly Gyp had a picture of himself sitting naked on top of an elephant in the middle of the Ohio River, and he began to giggle! Suppose when he came to the other side, Queenie walked right smack into somebody's back yard! Nope, he'd better just wear his clothes over and let 'em dry afterwards, when he found a place to hole up for the day!

Carefully he waded out into the water. The thick mud on the bottom squeezed between his toes. He waded and waded, but the water didn't come any higher than his ankles. This must be the place all right; he'd heard people talk about the shallows at Crosstown, where a horse could walk right across and never get the saddle wet. If a horse could do it, an elephant surely could. Particularly, Queenie, the biggest elephant in the world!

Gyp raised his head to search for the other shore. It wasn't supposed to be more than a hundred yards across right here. Suddenly, as he looked, he heard a faint faraway sound. It was a rooster. Glory, it was pretty near morning! He'd have to hurry. "If we don't get across and hide some place before it's good and light, we're goners."

He ran back through the water, and scrambled up the bank. There was no time for picking his way this time. Gyp felt the sharp edge of a half-buried log rip through his pants leg into his skin but he couldn't stop. He found Queenie finishing the last of the peanuts. She looked interested in the rest of the bread. "Here, take it," said Gyp. "I'm not hungry. Now, Queenie, listen. I've found a good place for us to cross. You carry me and walk real careful, and before you know it we'll be in Kentucky again. We'll get to Paducah by Labor Day, sure as shooting, and we'll find Mr. Tom Jeffreys and tell him all about it. You'll like that, won't you, Queenie?" For a minute Gyp could see the tall, proud way Mr. Jeffreys sat on his white horse, Star. He heard the jingle of the silver harness, and watched the way Mr. Jeffreys leaned down to pound on Queenie's side: one-two; one-two-three. "Be a good girl, Queenie," he had said. "I'll come and get you on Labor Day."

"He will, too," promised Gyp, as he took a deep breath and hugged Queenie's trunk against him for courage. "I'll never let them take you off to Chicago to that zoo. You're a royal elephant, Queenie, and by daylight you're going to be walking the dusty roads of Kentucky, just like Mr. Jeffreys meant for you to do."

Gyp whistled softly. Down went Queenie to her knees. In an instant he had been swung up on her great head again, and they were off. "Go on, Queenie, this way," Gyp drummed on her right side, and Queenie obeyed. The shore looked different from up here than it did when he was walking. He hoped he didn't miss the place. There it was. There was the log he'd bumped into. Gyp put his hand down on his leg and felt the cut place. It wasn't bleeding very much, but it was sore.

"This is it, Queenie, right here. Now, down you go, but be real careful."

Queenie looked down at her feet. Then she looked at the water. From behind the woods on the other side of the river, pale pink clouds stained the grey sky. The Kentucky shore swam mistily beyond the dull water. For the first time Queenie realized exactly where she was and what she was about to do. She gave a little snort and stopped dead still. Queenie had no more idea of walking into the Ohio River than a rabbit!

"Queenie!" begged Gyp. "You've got to, Queenie. Come on, now, be a good girl, like Mr. Jeffreys said." Queenie didn't move. Gyp clamped his teeth together hard to keep back a sob. "Oh, Queenie, what'll we do! We've got just a little while before daylight. Then they'll catch us, sure!" He slid to the ground and scrambled down the bank.

"Look, Queenie, look at me! It's all right, see? I wouldn't tell you so if it was too deep. Come on, Queenie, try it!"

Queenie put out one foot on the edge of the bank. It sank into the half-baked clay, and then

held firm. She tried another step. Gyp went back
to encourage her. He doubled up his fist and beat
on her side: one-two; one-two-three. "Good girl,
Queenie, I knew you weren't afraid. See, I'll stay
right alongside you. Here's the water now. Just
keep on going. It's real shallow for a long ways."

Slowly, cautiously, as if it were against her
better judgment, Queenie walked into the river. It
was cool and pleasant, after the dusty trip, and
Queenie suddenly found she liked it. Gyp couldn't
walk fast enough to keep up with her. The water
was up to his knees and dragging at his pants leg.
There was still a lot of current over these sand
bars. Like walking, walking, in a dream and not
getting anywhere.

"Stop, Queenie, stop. You've got to carry me on
your trunk. There's always lots of holes in the river,
and I'm scared I'll step into one." Queenie curled
her thick trunk up into a sort of swing, and Gyp
settled himself in it. He wrapped one arm around
the trunk, and balanced himself as they started off
again. This was better. Like sitting in a wash tub
with all your clothes on! Only the wash tub was
powerful big, and getting fuller and fuller.

Suddenly Gyp didn't like the feeling of sitting
there, with the river almost up to his chin. "I'm going to stand up, Queenie," he said, "just you keep

on going. We're more than half way across now; it's not going to get much deeper." But no sooner had he said those words than Queenie stepped into a hole! One minute she was on firm bottom, with the water to her knees. The next there wasn't any bottom at all. Queenie "histed" her trunk and that left Gyp floating!

CHAPTER FOUR

FOR ONE awful minute Gyp thought he was going to drown! What was worse, he thought Queenie was drowning, too. Now, nobody would ever know why he ran away with her, and Mr. Tom Jeffreys would think he was no better than Mr. Catfish Williams! When that terrible thought hit Gyp, he decided he'd better start swimming, and he did!

The first thing he bumped into was Queenie. Queenie had started swimming, too, but she had to hist her trunk above the water to get air while she swam. That's why Gyp had lost his seat. The Ohio

40

River can change over night, so you never know
where the holes are. Gyp grabbed at Queenie and
caught hold of her funny whip of a tail. He held
on for dear life and shouted, "Go on, Queenie, keep
swimming! We'll hit the shallows again soon. Don't
be afraid!"

Queenie may or may not have been afraid, but
she didn't waste any time getting over. Water was
all right, but enough was enough. It didn't take
long before she was on the sand bar again, and
rose out of the water like Jonah's whale. Gyp
let go of her tail and stood up beside her. He
coughed and choked before he could get his
breath.

"Glory! That was a close one. Guess this old
river is on Mr. Catfish Williams' side. Just because
of his name! Come on, Queenie, let's get to shore.
I feel like a catfish myself."

When the sun came up a few minutes later, it
looked down upon a sight it had never seen before.
Many things have come out of the Ohio River,
from the days of the Indians and the first white ex-
plorers, but never before had an elephant and a
boy walked out of its muddy waters and up its
banks at dawn! The buzzards circling above the
willows wheeled away in alarm. The crash of
Queenie's mighty feet through the underbrush sent

every good Kentucky rabbit to its hole in terror.

There was no road leading up from the river. No sign of life or settlement anywhere along the bank. The current must have taken them downstream away from Crosstown.

"That's safer," said Gyp. He tried to wring some of the water out of his pants legs and shook the wet hair out of his face. Queenie was contentedly pulling elderberries off some tall bushes as if she knew she was back home.

"You don't look at home, though," said Gyp. "You sure don't look as if you belonged in these woods at all. If anybody sees you, they'll turn in the alarm, sure. Come on, Queenie, we've got to find a place to hide."

It isn't easy to hide an elephant! Particularly the biggest elephant in the world. Gyp and Queenie kept pretty close to the river bank, and headed toward Crosstown as far as they dared. Gyp knew there would be farms along the bottom lands pretty soon, and farms meant corn, and maybe hay, still drying in the fields. Mr. Jeffreys had said Queenie had to have a bale of hay and five bushels of oats a day. He didn't know where they'd find the oats, for that harvest was over, but the second hay crop and good sweet field corn would suit Queenie fine.

"But we daren't go for food till night time, or

somebody'll see us. And we better not go any further out of these woods. So come on, Queenie, let's stop here."

It was a perfect hide-out spot, sheltered from the river side, as well as from the farms. With the hot sun of the last Sunday in August pouring down, Gyp was sure Mr. Catfish Williams' narrow eyes could see them across the river if they were anywhere near the bank!

"They'll be looking for us by now, Queenie," he said, as he matted down some long grass for a bed.

Gyp took off his wet shirt and his torn pants and laid them in a patch of sun. He looked anxiously at the cut on his leg. It throbbed pretty hard, and looked kind of "angry." He tore a strip off his shirt and tied it around the place. Then he lay down. "Come on, Queenie. You better get some rest, too. You've had a hard night, and we've got a long way to travel to be in Paducah this time next week."

Queenie picked one last bunch of elderberries and tucked them, branch and all in her mouth. Carefully she looked over the spot Gyp had picked out, and walked around it once or twice to make sure it suited her. Then, with a grunt, she went down on her back knees, and rolled on her side beside him. If she had been two inches closer,

she would have squashed him as flat as a pancake!
Gyp grinned. He forgot his sore leg. He forgot
Mr. Catfish Williams, who was only separated from
them by a hundred yards of river. He forgot he was
hungry or bone-tired or scared of being hunted by
the law for stealing an elephant. All he could think
of was how much he loved Queenie.

"I'll take care of you. We'll find Mr. Jeffreys.
Don't you worry about anything," he said. He
doubled up his fist and reached up and pounded on
Queenie's tall side: one-two; one-two-three. In a
minute they were both asleep.

That was the beginning of the strangest three
days in Gyp's life. They hid by day, and walked by
night. Only they didn't get too far, because they
had to spend so much time finding food. The first
night when they woke up it was hard to know
where they were going in the strange dark. Gyp's
stomach was even emptier than Queenie's, because
he couldn't eat elderberries. Hunger made them
bold, so they left the shelter of the woods and
finally found a cornfield. It was second planting,
however, and not many of the ears were big
enough for eating. Queenie liked them all right,
but Gyp couldn't get much nourishment out of soft
cobs!

"We've got to find a place where people are liv-

ing, Queenie. Then they'll have a regular garden.
Maybe even some apple trees, or peaches."

Just before daylight, they did find a place. It was
a real nice-looking garden when they found it, but
by the time Queenie had walked in among the cab-
bages and okra, it didn't look quite so nice. Gyp
was sorry to have to mess things up so, but there
wasn't time to be careful. He pulled up an armful
of butter bean vines and gave Queenie a big watermelon to carry. Then they hurried back to the
cornfield and hid in the middle of it just as the
sun came up.

"Queenie," said Gyp, his mouth full, "if anybody
ever told me I'd like raw beans, I'd a thought they
were crazy. But these are the best beans I ever
ate in all my life! Someday we'll come back and
pay these people for their stuff. But first we have
to get to Mr. Jeffreys."

Gyp didn't rest very well that day. The sun
burned like a red-hot stove, and the grasshoppers
and gnats nearly worried him to death. His leg
began to hurt real bad and looked kind of swollen.
But the thing that bothered him the most was the
waste of time. It was Monday and only one week
before Labor Day. "We're still a good thirty miles
away from Paducah, Queenie. Mr. Catfish Williams will hunt for us on the other side for a day or

two, then he'll start thinking about the river and figure out where we've crossed. Our only chance is to get through Crosstown before people hear you're missing."

But by the time Monday night was over, everybody in Crosstown knew that something was missing! The first report came to Mr. Berry, the sheriff, about Monday noon. Old man Wilson said a herd of wild horses had trampled the late corn in his river-bottom acres. The widow Allen reported a gang of boys had ruined her garden: "Just plain vandals, they were! Pulled my butter bean vines up by the roots!"

Along about nine o'clock, just after dark, the first of the "ghost" stories began to spread around town. The First Colored Baptist Church of Crosstown was having a baptizing down at the river, and just as the preacher finished the prayer, a huge grey "thing" rose right up out of the field and rushed past the congregation! It was so monstrous that the baptizing broke up in a panic. Two hours later, ten people had seen it. Sometimes it walked; sometimes it flew. People had seen its wings! It must have come straight from old Scratch himself, from the damage it did. Haystacks knocked down; fences pulled up. It seemed to have a preference for watermelon patches!

Gyp and Queenie were running into trouble. The closer they came to Crosstown, the more fences and fewer groves of trees they found. Of course, fences weren't any real problem, but Gyp hated to have to pull 'em up. Still, they just couldn't go all the way on the main road, and they had to keep an eye out for some place to hide when it began to get light. So all night, they kept skirting the north edge of town, always working a little further in, but never getting too close. When they'd come to a log fence, Queenie would unstack the logs just enough to let them walk through. But if it was a "bobbed wire" fence they'd have to pull up the posts. Gyp would say, "One, two, three—heave—!" and up would come the post Queenie was pulling on, and about two more each way along the wire!

Morning found them in the last cornfield on the edge of town, with a pile of sweet potatoes, an armload of roasting ears, and another watermelon. If it hadn't been for the melons, Gyp would have had a hard time. There weren't many places to find drinking water outside of people's wells, and they were mostly too close to the house for him to use.

Morning also found Mr. Berry, the sheriff, at his wits' end! "You've got to organize a posse, Sheriff, and catch this gang," said Will Hancock, the livery stable owner and Mayor of Crosstown.

"What if it *is* a ghost?" said Sheriff Berry, nervously.

"Fiddlesticks! Ghosts don't need to pull up fences. They go right through! Only a gang of men or an elephant could do this much damage in two nights. And since I never heard tell of elephants roaming wild in Kentucky, I say it's a gang of men. It's your duty to find 'em."

"I will, I will," said Sheriff Berry. "I'll make you a deputy, Mayor, and we'll set a trap for 'em tonight."

That was Tuesday night and the time that Gyp had decided to try to get through town. He longed to hit the good hard road from Crosstown to Paducah. He had traveled it so many times that he knew every turn and every ditch. It wouldn't be hard to make time on that road at night, or to find places to hide by day. When they got to the old picnic grounds outside of Paducah, he'd leave Queenie, if he could find a rope or a chain to tie her, and he'd hike fast into town and find Mr. Jeffreys. No trouble finding the biggest man in Paducah! His newspaper office on Main Street, or his Dixie Bee Café; they could always tell him where Mr. Jeffreys was, even if one of the

Jeffreys' Jewels Circuses wasn't in town. But it was bound to be, if he got there by Saturday. The three-ring Diamond Circus always played Mr. Jeffreys' home town for the Labor Day week end.

"Everything will work out fine, Queenie, once we're through this little town. Now listen. Here's our plan. Soon as it's dark, we start. We'll go into town along the cemetery, turn onto Main Street at the Methodist Church, and when I give you the signal, GO! It's only about six blocks. Go as fast as you did that night we left the circus, and we'll be out of town so fast they'll never know we were in it!"

Queenie swung her trunk at a mosquito, and stamped down another cornstalk. She was just as anxious to get to that open road as Gyp. Cornfields are no place for elephants, and Queenie knew it. She hadn't had a good taste of oats for three days.

Everything worked fine at first. The night was as dark as a pocket, with no sign of a star. Now and then a dull rumble of thunder threatened. Not a leaf stirred on the maples that lined the cemetery road. Gyp was riding on Queenie's back, to give his leg a rest, and to let Queenie have a better chance of speed, when they hit Main Street. Not a light showed in the houses as they passed.

It was too hot for lights. Those who hadn't gone to bed in Crosstown by ten o'clock of a Tuesday night were sitting on their porches in the dark, hoping for rain.

Mrs. Will Hancock was sitting on her porch, waiting up for her husband who had gone with Sheriff Berry to catch the gang. Suddenly she felt a sort of shudder go through the frame house. She strained her eyes to see what was passing on the road. "What in the world?" she said to herself. "The way the house shakes, you'd think an elephant was going past!"

At that very moment a jagged streak of lightning tore open the darkness just long enough for Mrs. Hancock to get a good view of Queenie swinging past her gate. Then it was dark again, and the thunder crashed in earnest. "Great day in the morning!" gasped Mrs. Hancock. "It IS an elephant!"

Queenie didn't like the thunder. Without any urging from Gyp she began to step out.

"That's the way, Queenie! That's the girl! Here we are at the corner. There's the Methodist Church. Now, here," he drummed on her right side with his heels, "here's Main Street, Queenie. GO! !"

Queenie went. The bricks of the one paved

street of Crosstown rang with the power of her running strides. To the two men waiting at the end of the street it sounded as if a locomotive had slipped its track and was rolling down Main Street.

"Will!" said Sheriff Berry. "Here they come! From the sound, there must be a dozen of them, horseback!"

"Never heard a dozen horses sound like that," said the livery stable owner. "More like a herd of elephants!"

CRACK! ! The lightning came again, this time so near and so bright that the whole length of Main Street was as bright as day.

"Sulphur and brimstone! It IS a herd of elephants!" yelled Sheriff Berry. "Stop. STOP! In the name of the law!"

At that moment the heavens opened and the storm began! What with the rain, and the thunder and the shouting of the men, both Gyp and Queenie were so confused and upset it's a wonder they didn't run right over Sheriff Berry and his Deputy! Gyp tried to quiet Queenie, who hated storms, and at the same time answer questions that he couldn't hear above the pouring of the rain. How they all got under the shelter of the carriage stand at the Courthouse, he couldn't remember. His leg was aching worse than ever, and his heart was like a cold stone with fear. Everything had been so near to working . . . and now . . .

Suddenly the rain stopped as sharply as it had begun. Sheriff Berry lit the lamps at the door of the Courthouse and looked unbelievingly at Gyp.

"It beats all! Dog take my buttons! Nothing but a kid and riding an elephant bareback down Main Street! Now start over. You say you're going to Paducah?"

Gyp kept patting Queenie's trunk. Her ears were fluttering open and shut, and she wasn't a bit happy.

"Yes, sir. To Paducah. I've got to get there by Labor Day, 'cause Mr. Tom Jeffreys is expecting Queenie."

"Queenie, huh? So this is Queenie? Pretty big for a little tyke to be riding around the countryside like this. If Mr. Tom Jeffreys is expecting Queenie, why don't he come and get her himself?"

Gyp's heart lightened a little. He was pretty sure this Sheriff didn't know anything about Mr. Catfish Williams or how he'd run away with Queenie. Maybe they could still get away.

"Mr. Jeffreys is a busy man. I'm taking care of Queenie for him. Is there any law against riding an elephant?"

Mr. Will Hancock was wet and sleepy and didn't like the look in Queenie's eye. "Sheriff," he said shortly, "this is ridiculous. There may not be a law against riding elephants in Kentucky, but there's a perfectly good law against running down farmers' cornfields and pulling up fences. There's also a law against scaring people out of their wits. I demand you put these two vagrants in jail and let me get on home and to bed, where I belong."

Gyp's heart sank again. Jail? Then they were lost.

"My jail's right in the back part of my house, Will Hancock. You know that as well as I do. I can't put this critter in my house."

"Never meant you to. Chain the elephant up in the back of my livery stable yard. I've got six good iron hitching posts and a length of chain."

Gyp had to lead Queenie across the street to Hancock's Livery Stable and help tie her up. His leg hurt so bad he didn't have any more fight in him. Besides that, he hadn't eaten all day.

"Don't forget to feed her," he told Mr. Hancock. "This is a royal elephant, the biggest and the smartest in the world. Mr. Tom Jeffreys would be pretty mad if anything happened to her."

"What does she eat?" said Mr. Hancock.

"A bale of hay a day and five bushels of oats."

"Is that all?" groaned Mr. Hancock. "Well, I can tell you one thing, Sheriff Berry. You hurry up and get this elephant out of here before I go bankrupt."

Gyp hugged Queenie's wrinkled trunk against his chest. "Goodbye, Queenie," he said, trying not to cry. "Be a good girl. We'll get along somehow, as long as we don't run into Mr. Catfish Williams. We've still got five days to get to Paducah."

"Five days!" said Sheriff Berry, who heard the last words. "At the rate you've been going, young man, you could plow up every cornfield in Kentucky in five days. You're not going to Paducah or anywhere else. You're coming home with me . . . to jail!"

CHAPTER FIVE

THAT WAS Tuesday night. Nearly midnight, by the time Sheriff Berry took Gyp over to his house and locked him in the little back room off the kitchen that served for the jail of Crosstown. Gyp was dead tired. He was starving hungry, too, because it was nearly twelve hours since he'd finished up the raw corn and the watermelon. But he fell across the cot in his cell and was asleep before he had a good chance to find out how hungry he really was.

He found out next morning, all right. It was already hot by the time he woke up. The sun was high, and pouring in through the barred windows of the room. Sheriff Berry had put a pitcher of water and half a loaf of bread inside the door and gone for the day. He had lots of people to see and lots of talking to do, to tell how he had captured a wild elephant single-handed, well . . . almost single-handed! It was evening before he remembered his prisoner and came to see Gyp.

"Glory, Sheriff," said Gyp. "I was scared you weren't coming back! Can I have my supper, please, sir . . . and I didn't have any dinner."

Sheriff Berry had just finished his second chicken dinner of the day. Half the people in town had asked him for a meal to hear the most exciting story that had ever happened in Crosstown.

He looked at Gyp apologetically. "I'm sorry, Sonny. Guess the time did slip by. I'm a bachelor, you know; don't have much in the house. Thought I left you some food this morning."

"Yes, sir, you did. Some bread. But I ate that. You see I haven't had much to eat since . . . that is, I'm pretty hungry."

"Well," said Sheriff Berry, "this is a jail, not a hotel. The law says bread and water, but I think I can find some cold side-meat and greens from yesterday's dinner."

Gyp ate them so fast he didn't even taste them. He was still starving hungry.

"Did you see Queenie? Is she all right? Did she get her bale of hay and her five bushels of oats?"

"She did. Saw to it myself, though Will Hancock kicked about the price. Said no elephant in the world needed that much food in one day."

"Oh, yes, she does. Mr. Jeffreys said so." Gyp wished somebody had laid down rules for feeding boys, as well as elephants! "Oh, Sheriff, please let me out! I've got to get to Paducah by Monday. I'll pay back every cent to the farmers for their corn and watermelons, if I have to work fifty years. Just let me and Queenie out to find Mr. Jeffreys."

Sheriff Berry looked unhappily at his prisoner. "I'd like to, Sonny. I really would. But the Mayor would throw a fit. Says there's something fishy about your story . . . doesn't believe it, and that's a fact. So, till we can find Tom Jeffreys I guess you'll have to stay right here."

Gyp couldn't keep the tears back any longer. He dug his fists in his eyes and turned his back to Sheriff Berry. It was no use. By the time they found Mr. Tom Jeffreys, Mr. Catfish Williams

would have found him. Then they'd never believe
him, against a grown man's word. The zoo man
would still have time to take Queenie, and he'd go
to jail, maybe forever!

"Sulphur and brimstone!" said the Sheriff, loudly.
"What've you gone and done to yourself?"

Gyp twisted around to see the back of his left
leg. It was puffed out and yellow, with red streaks
around the cut. "I hurt it. On a log."

"I'll say you did! Sit down and I'll get some hot
water and soak it for you. It don't take a doctor to
see a case of blood poisoning just hankering to de-
velop. You couldn't go to Paducah with that leg,
Sonny. So just take it easy, till Mr. Jeffreys shows
up."

Sheriff Berry really was a good-hearted man,
Gyp admitted to himself. He was in and out of his
cell during the night and all next day, putting hot
wet bandages on Gyp's leg, and patting him on
the back, and telling him he would soon be well
again. But kind words don't fill an empty stomach,
and Sheriff Berry just couldn't cook!

He either ate his own meals at the boarding
house or got invited out. There wasn't anything
but cornmeal and side-meat in his kitchen, and not
much of that. For two days Gyp ate bread and

drank spring water. By Thursday night he would have gladly given his healing leg for a full meal! He was so empty he could hear the water splash when he drank! He longed for Queenie, and he longed for some of Queenie's oats!

"If I ever get out of here," he whispered to himself, "I'll eat for a whole day . . . I'll eat everything that ever came out of a kitchen. I'll eat till I bust!" And he fell asleep to dream all night of fried chicken and blackberry cobbler.

All this time, Queenie was miserable, too. Oh, she had her bale of hay, and her five bushels of oats. But after the first taste on Wednesday morning, she didn't really care whether she had them or not. There was only one thing Queenie wanted. That was Gyp. She waited pretty patiently Wednesday night and Thursday morning. It was hot in the livery stable yard, and Queenie hated the hot sun on her skin. The horses for hire in the stalls kept up an awful neighing and stamping because of Queenie. They weren't used to seeing, or smelling, elephants in their yard! The stable man at Hancock's didn't like elephants any better than the horses did and every time he had to feed or water Queenie, he took an extra chew of tobacco to give him courage.

Queenie could smell the tobacco coming. She shuffled her feet restlessly and gave a little snort. It made her think of someone she didn't like, and that made her lonesomer for the one she loved.

"Look at that!" yelled the gang of boys who had sprung up like wild mustard all over the livery stable lot when the word got around about Queenie. "Look at her flap her ears and all! Bet you she could pull those hitching posts up like anything, if she had a mind to!"

"You kids git out of here!" said the stable man. "This ain't no circus. You'll rile this old elephant up, and then where'll we be? Now, skeedaddle . . . before I call Mr. Will!"

He watched the boys drag themselves off the lot and wait at the end of the street. He knew they would be back the minute he went in the stable. "Elephants!" he said, bitterly. "What kind of a livery stable did this turn out to be? I never hired out to be jailer to an elephant!" And he spat a great stream of tobacco juice at the hard-baked ground.

The effect of that action on Queenie was more than the boys had hoped for! Up went those big ears! Slash went the big grey trunk through the air! Queenie's brain burned like fire with the memory of her first meeting with a man she loathed. She had no intention of standing there chained to four puny posts while she was insulted again. Angrily, she raised her huge feet, one, two, three, four . . . and with each upward thrust, the iron hitching posts pulled out of the ground like spring onions after a rain!

"She's loose!" yelled the boys, and rushed for the nearest trees! They peered down like monkeys to watch with excitement. There was plenty! People rushed out of their stores, somebody ran for the Mayor, the fire alarm was turned in, and within five minutes every one of the eight hundred people in Crosstown had collected within sight of Hancock's livery stable to watch the sights.

But Queenie had already calmed down. She was searching every face in the crowd, sure that Gyp would be there, somewhere, and come and take care of her. She even let them put another longer chain around one leg and fastened it to the blacksmith anvil inside the stable. It was long enough for her to walk around the lot, and she began a careful march, swinging her trunk and looking for Gyp. The crowd scattered. The boys climbed down from their trees in disgust at this tame ending, and Sheriff Berry wiped his forehead in relief.

"That was a close one," he said. "For a minute I thought we were going to have trouble."

"I've got plenty of trouble," said Will Hancock, looking at his torn-up hitching posts. "And I don't like any part of it. If I don't get some word from Tom Jeffreys by Saturday, I'm going to take matters in my own hands. I'll go across the river to that circus that's been playing over in Illinois. That man Williams used to come to Crosstown every summer. He didn't have any elephants with him, but he's bound to know something about animals. Maybe he can take this beast off my hands till Jeffreys shows up. A few more days like this and I'll be in the poorhouse!"

If Gyp had heard these words he never would have dreamed of anything Thursday night. He wouldn't even have slept. As it was, he woke up Friday morning feeling worse than he ever felt before in his whole twelve years!

Gone with his dreams were the chicken and blackberries! There on the floor was his water jug and another piece of cold corn pone. Here it was Friday, three days before Labor Day! He just had to get out of this jail and get Queenie to Paducah. His leg was pretty nearly well and he knew they could make it. "Sheriff Berry's on my side! He's just got to let me out. Even if I have to tell him about Mr. Catfish Williams . . . no, I can't do that. Oh, what'll I do? . . . Glory! What's that?"

That was a sound Gyp hadn't heard very often. It was a sound that sent chills running up and down his back. It was Queenie trumpeting . . . and there was rage in the sound. "Queenie," screamed Gyp, as if she could hear him, "Queenie, what's the matter? What are they doing to you?"

The sound of feet pounding, and people yelling came through the little window of Gyp's cell.

"Sheriff Berry! Sheriff Berry! Get your gun and come runnin'! The elephant's gone plumb crazy! She's tearing up everything in the livery stable! Mr. Hancock says you've got to shoot her!"

CHAPTER SIX

GYP RATTLED the bars of his window with all his strength! "Queenie, Queenie," he sobbed . . . then, "Sheriff, don't shoot her . . . you can't shoot her . . . let me out. I'll take care of her. . . ."

But there was no answer: only the shouting of the people, the slam of the front door, and a furious trumpeting from Queenie.

Gyp beat his fists together in terror. But he heard no shots, only a terrific crash, as if a roof had fallen in. He sat down on the edge of his cot, because his knees were too weak to hold him up any longer. What could have happened that would make Queenie go wild like that? There was only one person in the world that she really hated. Could Mr. Catfish Williams have found them already? Was he maybe over there right now with Sheriff Berry and the Mayor?

Suddenly the noises grew nearer and he heard a whole crowd coming up the steps and into the house. A dozen boys stuck their faces up to the bars of his window, and he heard Sheriff Berry hurrying to his door.

"Sonny," panted the Sheriff, his face red as a beet, "come along, Sonny, and take care of this elephant. She's wild as a coot and can't anybody stop her."

"You didn't hurt Queenie, Sheriff, did you?"

"Hurt Queenie? Queenie's the one doing the hurting."

"But your gun. Somebody said you were s'posed to shoot her."

Sheriff Berry looked down as if amazed to see that he still had his rifle in his hand. He broke open the barrel and tossed it across Gyp's bed.

"That gun won't kill an elephant. That's a squirrel gun! Ain't anybody round here with a gun that could kill an elephant, except to shoot her all over

and let her die by slow torture. I wouldn't do that
to a snake, much less an elephant."

"Oh, thank you, Sheriff Berry," said Gyp, weakly.

The Sheriff waved his arms impatiently. "Come
on, don't waste time thanking me. Can't you hear
what she's doing?"

One boy yelled through the bars of the window. "She picked up Mr. Hancock's buggy and
threw it right over the fence!"

"She smashed two spring wagons and walked
over the pieces!" screamed another in delight.

"Glory!" said Gyp, "that's terrible! What ever
would make her do that?"

"Nobody knows," panted Sheriff Berry. "The important thing now is to make her behave. Come
on, come on, there's no time to be sitting down."

But Gyp did sit down. He sat right down on his
cot and folded his hands as calmly as if he were in
church.

"No, sir, I'm not coming."

"Of course you're coming. It's your elephant,
and your fault. Now you get over there and make
her stop tearing up this town!"

"No, sir," said Gyp, politely. "It's not my elephant. You arrested me and Queenie and wouldn't
let me take her to her owner. You locked me up
and wouldn't let me out. And you haven't given

me anything but cornbread and water to eat for three nights and two days. You've been eating, but I've been starving. You take care of her."

Sheriff Berry was stumped. He left Gyp sitting there and went for Mayor Hancock. After all, it was Will Hancock's livery stable that was being torn up!

Five minutes later they were both back in the jail. Gyp still sat as cool as a cucumber on his cot. He got up politely when he heard the door slam.

"Boy," said Mayor Hancock, as white as the Sheriff was red. "What do you want? Why won't you come and quiet this elephant?"

"I'm hungry," said Gyp, simply.

"Is that all?" roared the Mayor of Crosstown. "I'll buy you the best meal in town! I'll buy you all you can eat! Just come and make this beast stop ruining my livery stable!"

But Gyp was already out of hearing. He ran like the wind. Out of the house, down to Main Street—past the Courthouse. At every step the noise was worse. At the livery stable lot he saw the last of a buggy wheel go sailing onto the roof of the stable.

"Queenie," he screamed, "Queenie, stop it! Behave yourself, Queenie. It's all right. I'm here, Queenie! It's me. It's Gyp."

The hurricane that was Queenie swung round at his voice. Her trunk stopped in mid-air; her ears wavered and drooped. Gyp ran straight to her and flung his arms around her trunk. He was crying and laughing and scolding all at once.

"Oh, Queenie, I missed you so! You bad girl, what ever got into you? Mr. Jeffreys would be ashamed of you. Queenie, I was so scared they would shoot you."

Queenie dropped her ears like a naughty puppy. It was funny to see anything that big act ashamed of itself. She looked around at the smashed wagons and pieces of buggy and shook her head sadly, as if she wondered who had done such damage.

Gyp turned around to find the crowd gazing at him in amazement from a safe distance. Even Sheriff Berry and Will Hancock didn't venture closer until Gyp called them.

"She's all right now, sir. She's real sorry. Did somebody tease her? I never knew her to act this way before." Then hintingly, "Maybe she was hungry, too."

"If anything can be hungry after eating all that," said Mr. Hancock bitterly, pointing to the tub of oats under a tree.

Gyp looked carefully at the oats. He scooped up

a handful, smelled it, then let it run through his fingers back into the tub.

"No wonder she got mad," he said. "There's tobacco in those oats."

There was a squeak and a rush, and the whole gang of boys turned and ran for their lives.

"Tobacco?"

"Yes, sir! Look for yourself. Somebody found out that Queenie hated tobacco, so they tried to make her mad by putting some in her food."

"It was those dratted kids," said the stable man. "I seen 'em hanging around just after I put out her food."

Mayor Hancock's face was something to behold. "I'll take care of them," he said. "There'll be a lot of worn-out switches in this town before nightfall."

"Yes, sir," said Gyp, "but what about me?"

"You?"

"I'm still mighty hungry," said Gyp.

And that was how it happened that a ragged, brown gypsy of a boy and the biggest elephant in the world walked down Main Street in Crosstown, Kentucky, at high noon on the last Friday of August.

They walked right up to the Dixie Bee Café, the best restaurant in town. There weren't any people inside because everybody, including the man who ran it, was walking down the street behind Gyp and Queenie! When they got to the double doors, Mr. Hancock pushed them open and said, "Go in."

Gyp went in. So did Queenie!

"Stop! Stop!" yelled the man who ran the Dixie Bee. "Good Lord, Mr. Hancock, you can't let that elephant go in my restaurant!"

"Are you going to try to keep her out?" asked the Mayor.

But Gyp had an idea. "Queenie's lonesome for me. She doesn't want to be left by herself any more. Maybe we could stay out here and eat."

So they did. Two people carried out a table and a chair and set it up on the sidewalk, right in front of the big glass window of the restaurant. Somebody else brought out an umbrella and opened it up and stuck the handle in the neck of the carafe of water in the middle of the table. Gyp sat down in the chair under the shade of the umbrella, and Queenie stood in the blazing white noon sun and was perfectly happy, because Gyp was right there with her.

While everybody watched, the waiter gave the menu to Gyp. He looked at it carefully, from the top line, BLACK-EYED PEA SOUP, right down the list:

FRIED CATFISH   SMOTHERED CHICKEN
SWEET POTATOES IN THEIR JACKETS
ROASTING EARS   STEWED OKRA
BUTTER BEANS   CABBAGE SLAW
SLICED TOMATOES
CUCUMBERS AND ONIONS
BISCUIT   LIGHT BREAD
PEACHES AND CREAM
BOILED CUSTARD   WATERMELON

And at the very bottom: FRESH BLACKBERRY
COBBLER.

"I'll take it all," said Gyp.

And he did. The waiter brought him everything
on that menu and put it all on the table at once.
Gyp ate every single bit of it, while the whole
town stood and watched him eat it! And Queenie
stood beside him, swaying happily from side to
side, and waving her big ears to keep off the flies.
Every once in a while, here would come Queenie's
trunk curling across the top of the table, and Gyp
would put a piece of biscuit or a little blackberry
cobbler in it, and Queenie would tuck it into her
mouth and give a little snort of happiness. Then
Gyp would reach up his doubled-up fist and beat
on Queenie's side: one-two; one-two-three. Never

was there a sight like that before or since in the State of Kentucky!

"If Mr. Jeffreys could see us now, Queenie!" said Gyp. "He'd be tickled." Suddenly there was a click. Gyp looked up to see a man pulling his head out of a black-hooded camera he had set up on the sidewalk.

"I got it!" said the cameraman. "Biggest picture of my career. I ought to get a raise out of old man Jeffreys for this picture!"

Gyp nearly dropped his third ear of corn. "Do you work for Mr. Tom Jeffreys?"

"Sure, he owns my paper in Paducah. The Dixie Bee is his chain of restaurants, too. There never was such publicity for a restaurant before."

Gyp's heart began to go like a trip hammer. He pushed back his chair and ran over to the man, who was folding up his tripod and getting ready to go.

"Listen, sir. Do you think Mr. Jeffreys might see this picture?"

"Everybody in Western Kentucky will see this picture. They'll carry it in every paper in the state after it comes out in Paducah tomorrow."

"Oh, sir, listen. This isn't just Mr. Jeffreys' paper and Mr. Jeffreys' Dixie Bee. This is Mr. Jeffreys' elephant, too. I've just got to find him. Will you help me?"

"Sure," said the man. "I'm catching the two-twenty into Paducah right now. Be there before suppertime. If Tom Jeffreys is in town I'll find him for you. If he isn't, he'll see this picture before noon on Saturday, don't you worry about that. I'll even put your name under it, so he'll know."

"That's the trouble," said Gyp. "He doesn't know my name. But he knows Queenie, all right. Just you say in the paper that I'm the boy who's taking care of Queenie for him till he comes to get her on Labor Day."

"I'll do it," said the cameraman. "One good turn deserves another. This picture is going to make my fortune. Goodbye, kid. Good luck."

Gyp watched him walk off toward the depot and his hopes went with him.

"We'll need luck, Queenie," he said, putting down the umbrella and starting to stack up his dirty dishes. "Mr. Jeffreys isn't the only one who will see your picture in the paper. Mr. Catfish Williams is probably a lot closer than Paducah by this time, and he'll not only recognize you, Queenie, he'll recognize me! We'll need a lot of luck, if Mr. Catfish Williams gets here first!"

CHAPTER SEVEN

THE WEEKLY edition of the *Paducah Sun* reached Crosstown on the noon trip Saturday. The Post Office always stayed open till people came for their papers, then it closed. This week all the rest of the stores in town closed, too. It was the big Labor Day week end.

For Gyp it was anything but a holiday. He had promised Queenie to get her back to Mr. Jeffreys by Labor Day, and now he couldn't. All he could do was sit and wait for something to happen to him. He felt in his bones it would be something bad.

"Cheer up, Sonny," said Sheriff Berry. He had brought Gyp's cot over to the livery stable so he could stay near Queenie. Nobody had suggested putting Gyp back in jail! They didn't bother to tie Queenie up again, either. She was as good and quiet as you please, now that she and Gyp were together. Even the horses didn't mind her standing inside the stable out of the sun.

"Take a look at this paper. We made the front page! If you look right there, where that stepping stone is, you can see my feet. They must have cut off the rest of the picture, but I'd know my shoes anywhere! You're famous now, Sonny! You've been in the paper!"

"Yes, sir. Has Mayor Hancock heard anything from Mr. Tom Jeffreys?"

"Nope. But I think I heard him say he was going to take a rowboat over to the Illinois side this afternoon, see if he could locate a circus fellow he used to know that would take you and Queenie along with 'em for awhile till Jeffreys comes around."

Gyp jumped up in terror! "Oh, no, he mustn't! You've got to stop him! Don't let him find Mr. Catfish Williams!"

"Why not?" said a deep voice behind them. "Don't you want him to tell me that you're not a good elephant boy after all?"

Gyp froze in his tracks. He had heard that voice only once before, but he could never mistake it. Slowly, with eyes lowered, he turned around. There stood a pair of boots, so polished he could see his own rags in them. Tucked in the tops of the boots were cuffs of fine white linen trousers. One strong brown hand was tapping a rolled-up copy of the *Paducah Sun* against the other, and the eyes that looked down at Gyp from Mr. Tom Jeffreys' proud tan face were full of reproach.

"Mr. Jeffreys! Oh, Mr. Jeffreys! You've come!"

"I certainly have. On the same train as this very interesting newspaper. Too bad I didn't come a little sooner, before you tore up the countryside mistreating my animal. I guess I didn't size you up right, after all."

"Oh, no, sir! You don't understand. I was taking care of Queenie, like you told me to. I had to run away with her before they could take her to Chicago!"

Mr. Jeffreys frowned. He turned to Sheriff Berry. "What's the straight of this, sir? Do you know how this boy happened to have possession of the most valuable elephant in the whole United States?"

Sheriff Berry opened his mouth once or twice before he could answer.

"All I know is what it says right in your paper. This elephant and Sonny here came a-riding down Main Street in the middle of a thunder storm last Tuesday night and they've been here ever since. He kept saying it was your elephant, and he had to take her to Paducah to find you by Labor Day. Something about a promise he made to get her there."

"He never made me any promise," said Tom Jeffreys slowly. "He never said a word to me in his life."

"I'm sorry to hear that," said the Sheriff. "Will Hancock didn't think much of his story, either. But I kind of thought Sonny here was telling me the truth."

Gyp's throat was so tight he could hardly speak. "I never spoke to you before, but you spoke to me. You said I'd make a good elephant boy and I should take care of Queenie. When you told Queenie goodbye you said you'd come and get her on Labor Day. I was only trying to have her there for you when you came."

"No boy your size could bring Queenie all the

way to Paducah! That was your father's job!"

It was too much for Gyp. After all his troubles and his hopes, nobody would believe him. Not even Mr. Jeffreys.

He began to cry. "He's not my father. He's mean and spiteful and he hated Queenie! He hated you, too; that's why he sold Queenie to the zoo in Chicago. I had to run away that night or it would be too late. You don't have to believe me, if you don't want to. Nobody believes me, but Queenie!"

The sound of her name carried inside the stable. There was a rumble of wooden planks and there, framed in the stable door, stood Queenie. Gyp ran towards her, still crying. His last hopes were shattered. It was more than he could bear. Throwing himself against the huge elephant's trunk, he sobbed as if his heart would break.

Queenie was worried. She curled her trunk around Gyp's shaking shoulders and rocked him gently. She made little snuffling sounds to comfort him. She did everything but tell him to hush crying and tell her what the matter was!

"Look at that!" marvelled Sheriff Berry. "That Queenie thinks she's Sonny's own mother, the way she loves him. If you could have seen him quiet her down yesterday I think you'd be inclined to believe the boy's story."

Tom Jeffreys knew as much about people as he did about animals. He could recognize devotion when he saw it. Queenie had never been hurt by this boy. Quickly he made up his mind.

"Queenie!" he called.

Queenie stopped her rocking. Gently she uncoiled her trunk and raised her head. When she saw her master across the livery stable lot she raised her trunk and trumpeted, but this time it was for joy.

She picked Gyp up as if he'd been a willow switch, and carried him across to Mr. Jeffreys. Like an overgrown mother cat showing off her kittens. Mr. Jeffreys threw back his head and laughed.

"Gyp," he said, "let's get your story straight. If Queenie's adopted you, you must be all right. Queenie never sizes 'em up wrong. Suppose you and the Sheriff and I find us a spot in the shade and start right from the beginning."

So Gyp did. He wiped his eyes and blew his nose and he told Mr. Tom Jeffreys everything that had happened since Queenie was unloaded from the No. 1 menagerie wagon of Jeffreys' Jewels. He told what Mr. Catfish Williams said about Mr. Jeffreys forgetting his old friends after he made a success, and how he looked at Mr. Jeffreys when he rode away. When he told about the tobacco juice

being squirted on Queenie's trunk, Mr. Jeffreys' eyes got as black as thunder.

"So that's why Queenie hates tobacco," Sheriff Berry whistled. "Can't say as I blame her. That Catfish feller must not have good sense. Don't he know an elephant never forgets a wrong?"

"But neither does Mr. Catfish Williams!" said Gyp. "He just waited all summer to find a way to get even with Mr. Jeffreys. None of the circus hands got any of their pay or a share of the profits. Mr. Catfish Williams doesn't really care about any-body."

"Didn't he take care of you?" asked Mr. Jeffreys.

"Oh, no, sir. I just lived with him. I took care of myself."

Gyp squared back his shoulders and looked straight at Mr. Jeffreys. Mr. Jeffreys looked straight back. Gyp's heart warmed at his words, "Yes, I be-lieve you did."

Then he got up and began to walk up and down. "What I can't believe is that he actually meant to go through with that sale! Catfish is a little shady sometimes, but he's never been outside the law. And stupid besides. How did he think he could get away with such a thing?"

Sheriff Berry looked interested. "Sounds pretty shady, no matter what he figured. I'd like to meet this Catfish feller. Anybody with a name like that's likely to be quite a character."

Suddenly he squinted against the sun and pointed to a horse and buggy turning onto Main Street from the river road. "There comes Will Hancock now. Looks like he's got somebody with him, two somebodies, in fact. Guess he must have found the feller he was looking for."

Gyp was terrified. "Get Queenie away from here! I've got to get her away before they see her. He'll take her back and I'll never take her to Padu—" He stopped short and looked at Mr. Jeffreys and grinned. "Glory!" he said, "I forgot you were really here."

Mr. Jeffreys moved fast. "Just keep on forgetting it, Gyp. Forget you've been talking to anybody. I'll just step inside the stable with Queenie. You stay where you are, and let the men do the talking. I'd like to do a little listening myself."

Gyp could feel his knees shaking as the buggy came closer. Mr. Hancock had to use one of his for-hire buggies from his livery stable, because Queenie had smashed his own to smithereens. It wasn't a very good buggy, and Mr. Hancock was hot and cross, with two other men squeezed in the seat, one of them just as cross and the other one fat. Gyp decided he'd better sit down. The buggy rolled up to the livery stable lot and the three men jumped out.

"That's him!" said Mr. Catfish Williams. He went back for the buggy whip and started for Gyp. "I knew it the minute I picked up that paper. You little thief, I'll wear the skin off your back! Where's my elephant?"

Gyp clamped his teeth together tight to keep them from chattering. He threw up both arms to keep the whip off his head, but Sheriff Berry pulled it away and tossed it on the ground.

"Here, here—just a minute, here! What's this all about, Will Hancock?"

The Mayor was tired. He was tired of the whole business. "It's like I told you, Sheriff. This boy was telling us stories. That elephant belonged to Williams' circus. He'd sold her to the representative of the Chicago Zoo," he motioned towards the little fat man, "but in the middle of the night the boy stole her and ran away."

"I couldn't believe it," said the fat man. "Imagine stealing an elephant! I hope she isn't hurt in any way. I'd hate to have to lose her again, after all this chasing."

"There's absolutely nothing the matter with that elephant," said Mr. Hancock, "except she's just too big. The freight train goes through at midnight. I'll be thankful to see her get aboard."

Gyp had to speak. He almost shouted the words so they could be heard good and clear. "You're not going to sell Queenie after all, Mr. Catfish Williams? You can't do that?"

"Why can't I, I'd like to know? You keep out of this! I'm sellin' this elephant, and then I'm swearin' out a warrant for your arrest. I'll see you go to the reform school where you won't do any more stealin'."

"Mr. Williams!" the little fat man sounded shocked. "I thought this was your son. Don't you think you're being a little harsh?"

"He's no son of mine! I've fed him and clothed him for years and he's never done a day's work. Now he pays me back by stealin' and lyin' and tryin' to get me into trouble. I'll be glad to see the last of him, too."

"I don't blame you, Catfish. He might be quite a nuisance once he began to talk." The words came from the door of the stable. The four men whirled around. There stood Queenie and Mr. Tom Jeffreys.

"Did you hear him, Mr. Jeffreys? Did you hear him say it? He still was going to sell Queenie, just like I said!"

"I heard him, Gyp. I heard a lot of things. Enough to tell me all I need to know."

"Tom!" whispered Mr. Catfish Williams. "Why, Tom, I didn't know you were in Crosstown."

"That's right, Catfish. I was supposed to be in Paducah, wasn't I? On Labor Day, when I was coming to get Queenie. Well, I saved you a trip, Catfish. Gyp here saved Queenie a trip, too."

He looked at the little fat man, who was staring with his mouth wide open. "I'm sorry, sir, to disappoint you, but this elephant is not for sale. She never was for sale. She's a royal elephant and she's going to walk the dusty roads of Kentucky with the Jeffreys' Jewels' Circuses, not spend her life in a cage."

Gyp rushed over to Queenie and beat his fist against her side: one-two; one-two-three. "See, Queenie, I told you so! You'll lead all the parades, like you did with the kings and princes!"

Mr. Jeffreys looked at them for a minute, then he doubled up HIS fist and beat on Queenie's OTHER side: one-two; one-two-three. Queenie snorted happily and swung her trunk from one to the other in delight.

"Somebody has to lead Queenie. It looks like she's chosen you. How'd you like to join my circus? You'd have to go to school in winter quarters just like Queenie, but I reckon if she can stand it, you could, too."

"Oh, Mr. Jeffreys," said Gyp. "I'd rather be with you and Queenie than anywhere else in the whole world."

"What was that I heard about swearing out a warrant?" said Sheriff Berry, hopefully. "Seems to me there's a good case of attempted robbery that this Catfish feller'd have a hard time getting out of. Hey! Where's he gone to? Mayor, turn that horse around and help me catch that feller."

"I think his circus people will take care of him," said the little fat "zoo" man, with satisfaction. "They've already made him divide up the season's profits and I think they're through with Mr. Catfish Williams' circus for good."

"Let him go, Mr. Jeffreys," said Gyp. "Please let him go! It doesn't matter, just so he can't hurt Queenie any more."

"I guess you're right," said Mr. Jeffreys. "Well, that's about all we have to do here, I guess. Except maybe leave a little money with Sheriff Berry to pay for the corn and watermelons you two ate between here and the river. Wish I could have seen you at that baptizing!"

Gyp giggled. It was the first time he had laughed

for a whole week. "Queenie was the biggest ghost in the world," he said.

Mr. Jeffreys gave a whistle. Queenie turned her great head and looked at him. Then she grunted a little and dropped to her front knees. Gyp stepped on Queenie's trunk and . . . whish, he was up on her head and sliding back onto her shoulders.

"Well," said Mr. Jeffreys, "I guess we'll be going. There's another freight train, going south, not north, in a little while, and there's a boxcar reserved on it for us. We've got to get to Paducah before Labor Day, don't we, Gyp?"

"But, Mr. Jeffreys!" said Mayor Hancock. "What about my feed bill? One bale of hay and five bushels of oats for four days. And my broken buggy? And the two wagons that elephant smashed? Aren't you going to pay me for those?"

Mr. Tom Jeffreys stopped and looked at Mr. Will Hancock in a way that made Gyp glad he wasn't looking at him. "I am not. You had no business to chain up my elephant. You had no right to arrest my elephant boy, either. He promised to take her to Paducah by Labor Day and if you'd let him alone last Tuesday night he would have kept that promise."

Gyp sat up as straight as Mr. Tom Jeffreys and folded his arms like the elephant boys he had seen on Mr. Jeffreys' posters. He smiled at Sheriff Berry. He smiled at the little fat man and at the stable man. He didn't dare smile at Mr. Tom Jeffreys, for fear he'd cry. For the first time in his life he knew that he belonged to somebody.

"Get yourself another buggy, Mayor," went on Mr. Jeffreys. "You and the Sheriff drive down to Paducah on Monday for the Labor Day performance of Jeffreys' Diamond Circus, the No. 1 Jewel of the Greatest String of Circuses on Earth! Gyp will leave a couple of free tickets for you at the window. Come on, Queenie!"

So off they went . . . across Main Street . . . down Depot Street . . . and onto the freight car to Paducah.

And that is the story of the boy who stole the elephant.